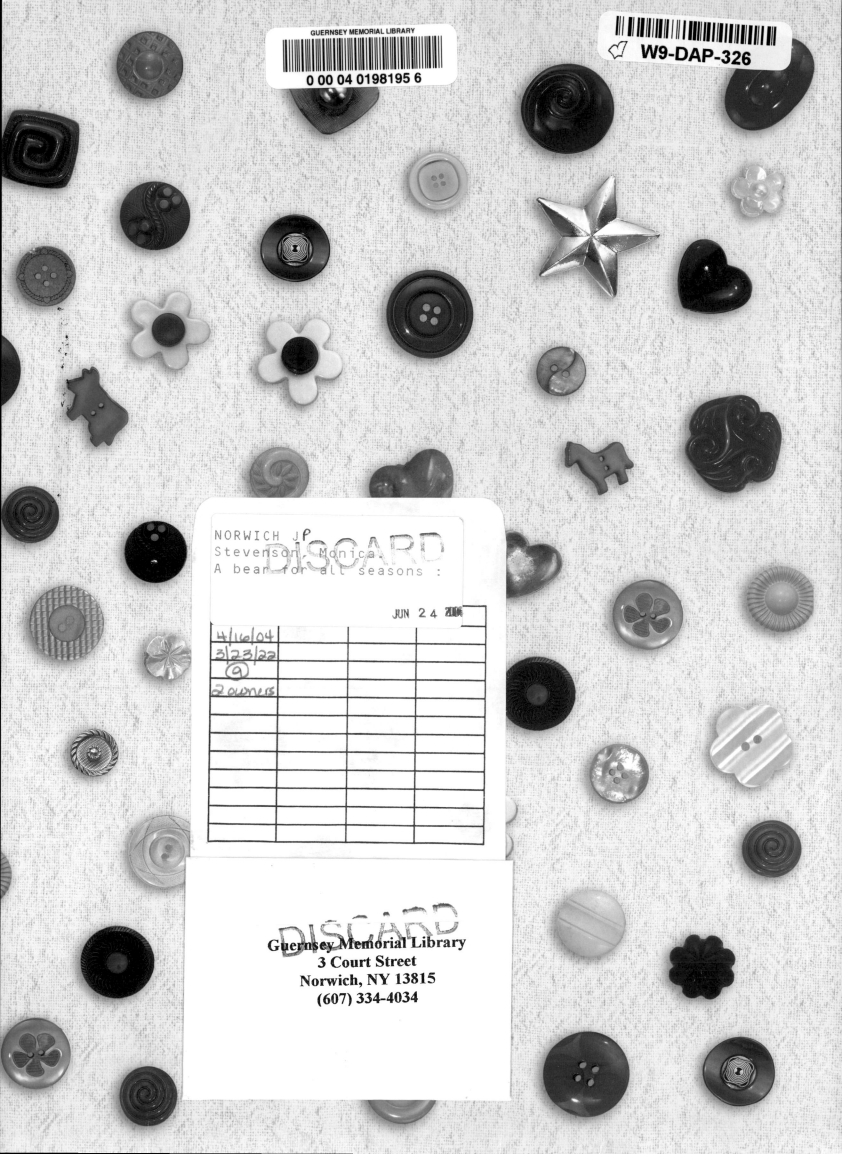

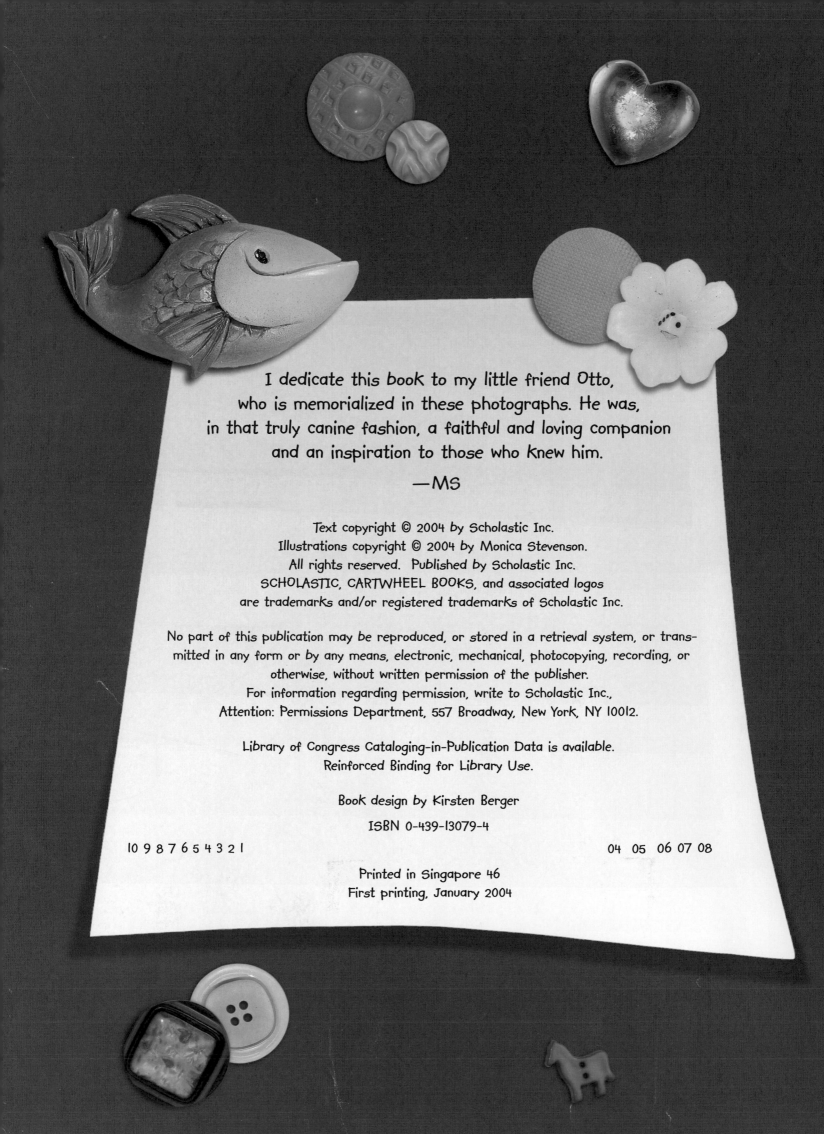

I dedicate this book to my little friend Otto,
who is memorialized in these photographs. He was,
in that truly canine fashion, a faithful and loving companion
and an inspiration to those who knew him.

—MS

Text copyright © 2004 by Scholastic Inc.
Illustrations copyright © 2004 by Monica Stevenson.
All rights reserved. Published by Scholastic Inc.
SCHOLASTIC, CARTWHEEL BOOKS, and associated logos
are trademarks and/or registered trademarks of Scholastic Inc.

Library of Congress Cataloging-in-Publication Data is available.
Reinforced Binding for Library Use.

Book design by Kirsten Berger

ISBN 0-439-13079-4

10 9 8 7 6 5 4 3 2 1   04 05 06 07 08

Printed in Singapore 46
First printing, January 2004

A BEAR FOR ALL SEASONS

The Kissenbear Family Scrapbook

Photo Illustration by Monica Stevenson

Cartwheel
B·O·O·K·S®

SCHOLASTIC INC.

New York   Toronto   London   Auckland   Sydney   Mexico City   New Delhi   Hong Kong   Buenos Aires

This is the first page
of the Kissenbear Family
Scrapbook. Here I am with
all the pictures to put in it.
There sure are a lot of them!
This could take a while.

Turn the page
and meet our family!

This is Daddy!
Mama says I'm
his "spitting image."
(Whatever that means!)

Here's Mama!
She's wearing her
favorite hat.

Here's my little brother, Rudy. He's the best ball player on the mountain!

This is me! Tag-a-long B. Kissenbear. Everyone calls me Tag.

This is Claudine, my big sister. We play board games together, and sometimes I let her win!

These are our pets. Our horse's name is Jupiter, our cat is Clementine, and the dogs are Otto and Stella.

That's our house over there.
Isn't it pretty?
I think it's the best house
in the whole world.
That's because it's
on Moon Mountain.

Crescent Village
Luna Forest
Moon Mountain

FIRST IT WAS SPRING

I love it when spring
is here! No more winter coats
and hats. When the rain falls,
it makes big puddles.
I jump in them and
— SPLASH! —
water goes everywhere!

My daddy wrote this
next poem about spring.
(I told him to add the part
about the puddles!)

ON MOON MOUNTAIN

A Song to Spring

Oh, spring, you're so springy.
How everything grows!
Your grass is a carpet
that tickles my toes.

Your flowers are sweet,
like a jar of fresh honey.
Your breezes are warm
when the morning is sunny.

You call the birds home
to build their new nests.
But your puddles that come
from the rain are the best!

Vacuum cleaners sure
can pick up a lot of stuff.
Sorry, Clementine!

Mama said it was time for a little
spring cleaning. Even Otto and
Stella got to work!

Otto sneezed about a gazillion times
when Daddy cleaned our chimney.

Mama says rain is nature's way of giving a drink to the flowers. They sure were thirsty that day!

I showed Claudine my super-secret baseball swing—and she used it to help Mama beat the dust out of our rugs.

No, no, Stella! That lemonade is for Mama!

Whew! Spring cleaning is a lot of work.

I'm glad it only comes once a year!

NEXT CAME

Summer is so much fun!

Mama lets me stay up a whole hour later. Last summer, I caught six fireflies, two frogs, and one green lizard!

My daddy wrote a poem about our summer.

SUMMER

We Love Summer

How do we love summer?
Oh, let us count the ways!
We love the stream
with its leaping fish.
We love the sun's warm rays.

In summertime, the fireflies shine,
while frogs *ribbit-ribbit* at night.
But the bees in the heat,
making honey so sweet—
now, *that* is the loveliest sight!

These are pictures from our
Moon Mountain Go-cart Race.
Our friend Edgar brought Jupiter
his favorite snack — a carrot!

Rudy's go-cart looked like a big cat.
Clementine was scared to get in at first,
till she saw it was only made of wood.

That's our friend Moose
washing my go-cart.

Stella and Clementine helped, too!

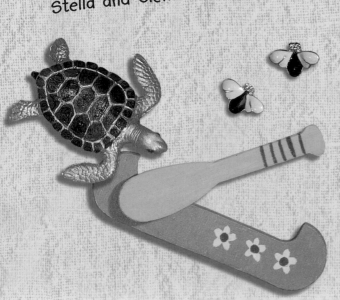

This is Claudine's friend Thomas.
The day before the race, they
worked on her go-cart all afternoon!

Say, "Cheese!" Mama takes a picture of me next to my go-cart. I named it the Flying Fish.

Are fish faster than cats?

Rudy won! He came in first place! (I guess cats are faster than fish.)

Here is Rudy, crossing the finish line!

That was the best day of the whole summer.

FISH
HONEY
$\frac{2}{2}$
$+\frac{2}{4}$

I bet I could fill this whole scrapbook just with things I love about fall— jumping in piles of leaves, helping Mama bake her honey apple cake, going on hayrides, and my most favorite thing, Halloween!

When Daddy reads his Halloween poem, he always lets me say the BOO! and WHOOO? parts!

WAS FALL

Fall Is Halloween

When the leaves turn to gold,
and the breezes grow cold,
you know that fall is here.
And what fall night
always gives us a fright?
Halloween! That one night of the year
when ghosts say BOO!
and owls say WHOOO?
and the moon is full in the sky.
And we all pretend to be
something else, as you'll see
when we come parading by!

Mama sewed this fish costume for Claudine.
She got to glue the eyes on the head.

This Halloween, I dressed as
a giraffe. It took me a while
to figure out how to walk
in the costume!

That's Daddy and Mama dressed as opera singers.
I didn't know what opera was, so Mama sang some for me.
Boy, was it loud!

Moose's violin was kind of squeaky, but Edgar and Thomas didn't mind. They love to dance!

Even Otto, Stella, and Jupiter got dressed up.

Here's Rudy dressed as a knight. His shiny helmet clanked the whole way down the mountain.

Happy Halloween!

SOON IT WAS

Here are the cold things I love about winter: building snow bears, ice-skating on the lake, and catching snowflakes on my tongue.

Here are the warm things I love about winter: baking cookies while Daddy reads to me, sitting by the fireplace, and drinking Mama's honey apple cider. (Yummy!)

Daddy wrote a poem about winter.

WINTER

Winter Snowflakes

Drippy, droppy snowflakes,
falling on the trees
turn the green to shiny white
as the branches freeze.

Snowy, blowy snowflakes,
piling on the ground.
Reach up high, touch the sky.
There's magic all around.

Winter snowflakes decorate
our mountain every year.
Drippy, snowy, droppy, blowy.
We love winter here!

This is the day we all made snow sculptures.

Claudine and Mama helped, too.
They used brooms to sweep snow
in piles for our snow bear.

Stella and Clementine wanted to help
shovel snow for our sculptures,
but their tongues kept sticking
to the icy shovels!

This is our snow bear in the moon!
I think we did a great job.

Rudy made this snow acorn all by himself!

Edgar surprised Thomas and Rudy
when he popped out of this pile of snow.

He was colder than a popsicle!

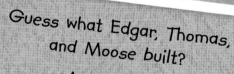

Guess what Edgar, Thomas,
and Moose built?

A snow bee.
(The flower was my idea!)

I wanted to put our snow bear in the freezer until spring came, but Daddy said it wouldn't fit.

At least we have this picture to remember him by!

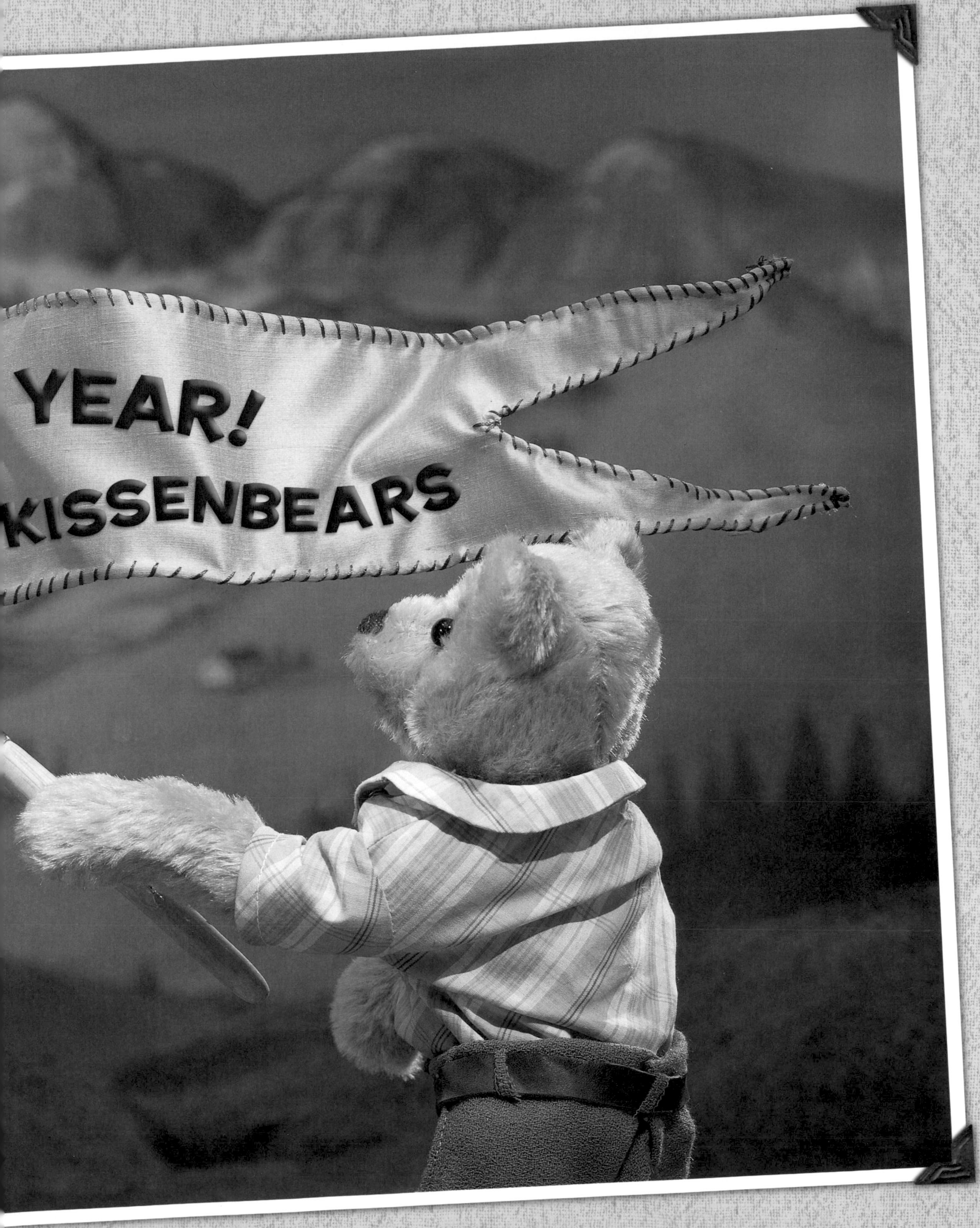
YEAR!
KISSENBEARS